DATE DUE

MUMMY RIDDLES

Katy Hall and Lisa Eisenberg

pictures by Nicole Rubel

Dial Books for Young Readers • New York

Dial easy-to-read

Published by
Dial Books for Young Readers
A Division of Penguin Books USA Inc.
375 Hudson Street
New York, New York 10014

The Dial Easy-to-Read logo
is a registered trademark of
Dial Books for Young Readers,
a division of Penguin Books USA Inc.
® TM 1,162,718.

Library of Congress Cataloging in Publication Data
Hall, Katy.
Mummy riddles/by Katy Hall and Lisa Eisenberg
pictures by Nicole Rubel.
p.   cm.
ISBN 0-8037-1846-2 (tr.)—ISBN 0-8037-1847-0 (lib.)
1. Riddles, Juvenile. 2. Mummies—Juvenile humor.
[1. Mummies—Wit and humor. 2. Riddles.]
I. Eisenberg, Lisa.
II. Rubel, Nicole, ill. III. Title.
PN6371.5.H3486   1997
818'.5402—dc20   94-37525   CIP   AC

First Edition
1 3 5 7 9 10 8 6 4 2

The paintings are made with black ink and colored markers.

Reading Level 2.3

*EASY
READER
E
H
11/97*

To mummies everywhere
K.H. and L.E.

To my mummy
N.R.

Do mummies enjoy being mummies?

Of corpse! Of corpse!

What do you call a mummy
that sleeps all day?

Lazybones!

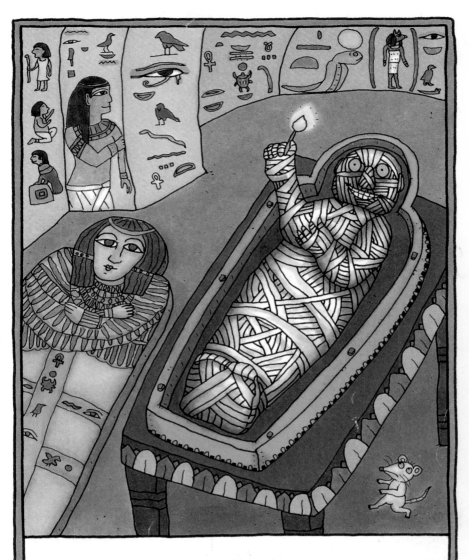

Where was the mummy
when the lights went out?

In the dark!

What does a mummy
take for a chest cold?

Coffin drops.

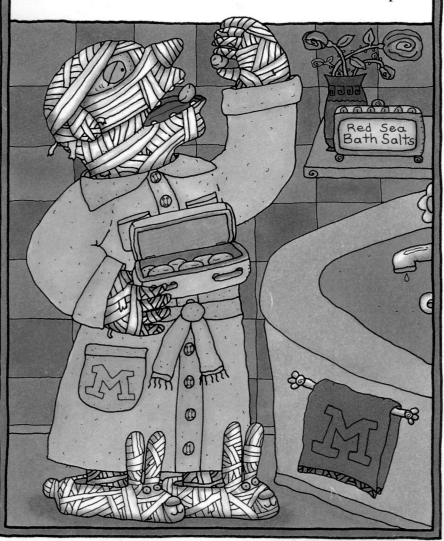

What's the speed limit
in Egypt?

55 *Niles* an hour.

What did the mummy
wear on Halloween?

Mask-ing tape.

What do mummies eat for breakfast?

Shrouded wheat.

What happened when
the boy mummy met
the girl mummy?

It was love at first fright!

Who belongs to the
Pyramid PTA?

Mummies and Deadies.

What sign did they hang
on the pyramid?

"Satisfaction guaranteed or double
your mummy back!"

16

How do mummies like
to eat their eggs?

Petri-*fried!*

What kind of music does
a mummy like best?

Anything with a *rag*-time beat.

What game do mummies
like to play?

Casketball.

What would you do
if you saw three mummies
walking toward you?

Hope it was Halloween!

What is a mummy after
he is 3,000 years old?

He's 3,001 years old!

What do you say about
a terrible mummy movie?

"It really sphinx!"

Where do mummies like
to sit at the movies?

Dead center.

What did the little mummy say
when the shopkeeper
gave him the wrong change?

"Egypt me!"

Does the mummy football
team lose many games?

No, they always tie up the score.

Why didn't the mummy
want to go out dancing?

He was dead on his feet!

What did the mummy
say when he got angry
with the skeleton?

"I have a bone to pick with you."

What happened when
the little mummy told a lie?

He was sent to his tomb!

Why did the mummy take her son to the doctor?

He had a bad sar-*cough*-agus!

What did the mummy
say when he looked
into the mirror?

"Who's the pharaoh of them all?"

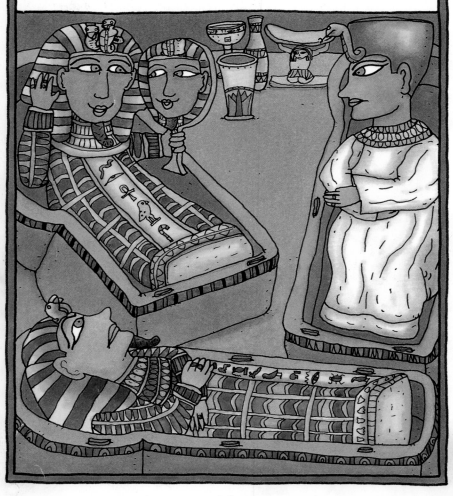

Why did the mummy leave
his tomb after 4,000 years?

He thought he was
old enough to leave home.

What do you say
to a hippie mummy?

"Like, wow, Deady-o!"

When do mommy mummies
get gifts?

On Mummy's Day!

Why couldn't the mummy
answer the telephone?

Because he was tied up.

What does a mummy call
the small rivers that flow
into the Nile?

Juve-niles.

How can you tell when
a mummy is angry?

She flips her lid!

How do mummies like
to drink their coffee?

De-*coffin*-ated!

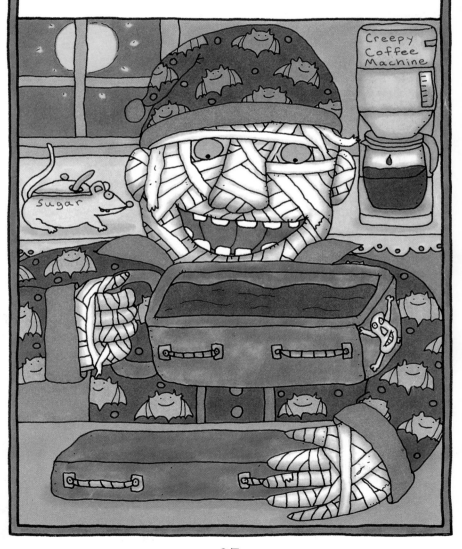

How does a mummy speak?

In a grave tone of voice!

What did the doctor
tell the little mummy
at her checkup?

You grue-some!

Where do mummies
like to go boating?

On Lake Eerie!

How can you tell
when a mummy has a cold?

She starts coffin!

Where do mummies swim?

In the Dead Sea!

What did the boy mummy
say to the girl mummy when he
took her out of her tomb?

I really dig you!

What did the daddy mummy
say to the little mummy when
she asked for some candy?

"But you just had
some candy a century ago!"

What do mummies
like to talk about?

Old times!

What do mummies
like to listen to?

"Wrap" music!

What should you do
if a mummy
rolls his eyes at you?

Roll them back!

Why was the mummy sent into the game to pinch-hit?

So he could wrap it up!